3 9077 08059 1327

P9-CSA-167

randomhousekids.com

ISBN 978-0-7364-3610-6

Printed in the United States of America

10 9 8 7 6 5 4 3 2

Disney

ZOOTOPIA

THE STINKY CHEESE CAPER

AND OTHER CASES FROM THE ZPD FILES

By Greg Trine
Illustrated by Cory Loftis

Random House 🏠 New York

THE STINKY CHEESE CAPER

The city of Zootopia was usually very safe. Animals of all different shapes and sizes lived there in harmony. Occasionally a problem would pop up, like the savage animal attacks from a few months earlier. But Judy Hopps and her partner, Nick Wilde, would catch the bad guys. As the first bunny and fox cops on the Zootopia police force, they liked proving that in Zootopia, anyone could be anything.

One afternoon, Judy and Nick were on traffic duty. A teen wolf named Wulfric had just been in a fender bender.

He had a brand-new license from the Department of Mammal Vehicles, and he seemed to have forgotten some rules.

"You really shouldn't operate a motor vehicle with your head out the window, Wulfric," Judy told him.

"I can't help it," Wulfric said. "Ever since Wild Times opened that new ride where the wind blows in your face, I want to feel that all the time!"

Judy shook her head. "This is the third time this month someone has blamed the Wind Tunnel for a car crash. Nick, we'll have to go by Wild Times and make sure the amusement park has a warning on that ride."

The fox nodded. Just then, Judy's radio squawked. Nick took over Wulfric's paper work so Judy could talk to Clawhauser. He was the cheetah who worked the front desk at the ZPD.

"I'm here, Clawhauser. Got another speeder for me to catch?" Even though Judy and Nick had solved one of the ZPD's biggest cases, Chief Bogo kept them working traffic.

"Nope. There's been a robbery at the Chez Cheez warehouse just outside Little Rodentia!"

Judy's ears twitched, which always happened when she was excited. "You can tell the chief we're on it!"

Clawhauser paused. "Hopps . . . some cops are saying you two got the case because no one else wants it. I hear it's a"—he lowered his voice—"stinky cheese robbery."

"It's all right, Clawhauser. Nick and I can handle it." They knew that police work sometimes came with smelly places.

After finishing with Wulfric, Judy told Nick about the robbery. Chez Cheez catered mostly to the residents of Little Rodentia, an area of the city where rodents such as mice, shrews, and hamsters lived. The restaurant also had a huge warehouse. It held large slabs of cheese that were shipped all over Zootopia.

Once she filled him in, Judy and Nick drove toward Little Rodentia. Near the edge of the bay, they took a detour around a construction site. "What's going on there?" Judy asked, pointing to the cement trucks.

"New bridge over the bay," Nick said. "The press is calling it the Bridge to Everywhere. Outbackers aren't too happy." He pointed to a small group of kangaroos and wallabies holding picket signs. "They're calling it the Bridge to Everywhere Except Outback Island." Even though Nick looked like he didn't care, Judy knew that her sharp-witted friend paid attention to every detail.

Judy parked the squad car outside the warehouse and went inside. Nick wasn't behind her. "Come on," she told her partner. He was leaning against the car, looking slightly green.

"Don't you smell that?" Nick asked, his nose wrinkling.

She sniffed. "It's just cheese. Not pleasant, but not stinky enough to stop me from doing my job." She pulled his arm and he followed her, covering his nose.

The manager of the warehouse was a rat named Vince. He met them at the door and led them to a back room with

a large, empty table. The smell was so strong now, even Judy had to cover her nose.

"The thieves came in through the back," Vince said. His whiskers fluttered nervously. He pointed to an emergency exit door that was propped open. Nick hurried outside for some fresh air—and to search for clues. Judy put some cheese crumbles in an evidence bag. Vince frowned but didn't say a word.

"Do you have any surveillance cameras?" Judy asked.

Vince shook his head as his whiskers continued to move. "Disabled. Whoever did this knew what they were doing."

Outside, Nick snapped photos of paw prints in the mud. He took one last breath of fresh air, then returned to the warehouse. "Got any idea why someone would want to steal this cheese?"

Vince nodded. "It's one of our top sellers. Losing it will hurt our profits this quarter. Even those scraps," he pointed to Judy's bag, "are worth more than my entire collection of hats."

"Is that why you're so nervous?" Judy asked.

He nodded. "The boss is going to have my tail for this."

"We'll be in touch," Judy said.

Back in the squad car, Judy started the engine and turned to Nick. "Any ideas?"

In the passenger seat, Nick plugged his phone into a laptop and uploaded the pictures of the paw prints. "If the cheese was really that expensive, that's a motive. Do you know what kind of prints these are?" He turned the computer toward his partner.

Judy squinted. "Too big for a rodent. Raccoon? Weasel?"

Weasel? They knew a thieving weasel. "Duke Weaselton!" they chorused.

Even if Duke Weaselton wasn't behind this theft, he knew the crime community better than anyone—even Nick, who used to be "legally adjacent" before he joined forces with Judy. "Know where we can find him?" asked Judy.

"Word on the street is he's found a

way to win some games at Wild Times. Let's check there," Nick said.

Judy drove while Nick sent his photos to the National Paw Print Database. As usual, there'd be a two-hour wait for the computer to identify the prints.

Wild Times was an amusement park that let the citizens of Zootopia explore their wild sides. Its newest ride, the Wind Tunnel, encouraged animals to stick their heads out of vehicle windows while driving.

As Judy and Nick entered the sprawling park, they blinked under the bright lights. Flashing signs advertised new games. Judy frowned as they passed the Wind Tunnel. A dingo was in the

back of the line. He slunk away when he saw her. *Good,* Judy thought, *one less accident for me to worry about.*

Nick had spotted Duke Weaselton and quickly cornered him. "This better be important, Wilde," Weaselton said.

"There's been a robbery at Chez Cheez warehouse," Judy said. "Have you heard anything?"

Weaselton froze, fear flashing over his face. Nick held him against a nearby pillar. Weaselton was good at weaseling out of being questioned by the police.

"Aha!" Judy exclaimed. "So you do know something!"

"Don't tell Mr. Big!" Weaselton replied, looking for an escape. "He doesn't like me near Chez Cheez. But . . . I wasn't. I was at a different warehouse in the area last night. I was meeting a contact about some giraffe scarves—nothing to do with cheese! A speeding sports car almost ran me over. It smelled bad, too."

"Could be our guy," Judy said to Nick. "Then what?" she asked Weaselton.

He shrugged. "Nothing. I jumped out of the way, yelled at the driver, and watched the sports car leave town on the Meadowlands Highway."

Nick and Judy let Weaselton go and headed back to their car. Nick scrolled through police reports, looking for anything about bad smells. "Bingo," he said. "The jail submitted a report. Turns out they had to evacuate the prisoners in solitary due to some bad smell on the west side."

"Good lead, Nick," said Judy. Maybe it wasn't the best lead, but it was the only one they had. They drove down the Meadowlands Highway to talk to the warden.

"Finally," said the warden. He was a jaguar with very good posture. "I've been waiting to talk to some detectives since I filed that report." He led Judy and Nick through the prison, past a bunch of empty cells. "Someone threw a huge piece of cheese over the wall. We had to evacuate this cell block."

"Solitary, right? How many prisoners were in there?" Nick asked.

"Yah. Just one. Only this beaver—I mean, platypus—who's been causing problems. Everyone's been mistaking him for a beaver, though. That gets him angry, and he whacks the other prisoners with his tail. It looks like a beaver tail, by the way."

Judy frowned. "Beaver tails are thinner and less furry. Really, the animals are very different."

"Close enough," said the warden.

Judy held back another comment. She wanted to tell him that knowing the difference between species was important, but they were here to solve a case. "Any witnesses?" she asked instead.

The warden nodded. "Me, actually. I was working in the tower last night. It was late . . . past midnight. A sports car drove up to the wall. Then someone got out and tossed the cheese over. Maybe he thought we don't feed our prisoners well enough."

"Did you get a good look at him?" asked Nick.

"A small wolf? Coyote?" He waved a hand at Nick. "Maybe even a fox. It was dark, and canines look similar."

Nick smirked. "Everyone thinks foxes are sly, but some of us are just trying to help our community."

"Thanks for your help," Judy said to the warden.

As she and Nick hurried back to the car, she exclaimed, "It makes no sense, Nick!"

But Nick wasn't listening. The National Paw Print Database had finally given them a match. "Turns out that paw print at Chez Cheez was from a dingo. That's odd—they're rarely off Outback Island."

"I saw one at Wild Times earlier," Judy said, putting the car into gear. "Maybe he'll know something."

Nick's fur bristled. "Or maybe he's our guy."

Judy thought that was a stretch, but

she didn't believe in coincidences. "Let's go find him," she said.

The dingo was back in line at the Wind Tunnel when Judy and Nick returned to Wild Times.

"That's a dingo, all right," Nick said when Judy pointed him out.

"Excuse me," Judy called to the dingo. "We'd like to—"

The dingo took one look at the officers approaching him and sprinted out the back door. "Innocent dingoes don't run!" Nick shouted. He tried to follow, but the dingo hopped into a fancy sports car and roared away.

"That's some car," Nick said as he and Judy ran for their squad car.

"We can catch him," Judy said. "He's been in the Wind Tunnel all day. I have a feeling he might have an accident soon."

Sure enough, the dingo only made it a block before his head popped out the window. A moment later, the car crashed. Judy and Nick squealed to a stop. The dingo pushed his door open and ran straight into the officers.

"Been stealing stinky cheese lately?" Nick asked. He took a sniff, and immediately his eyes started to water. "Never mind, I already know the answer. Judy, check the car."

Judy spotted cheese crumbles in the backseat. "Way to sniff out our guy, Nick."

The dingo frowned. "You don't have to make such a stink about it."

Judy and Nick took the dingo to the

station for questioning. He confessed to the theft. He'd wanted fancy cheese for a dinner party so he stole some. But he hadn't been able to stand the smell and threw it out the window. Nick and Judy didn't blame him.

"Good job," Judy said to her partner.

Nick gave her a high five. "Now let's get rid of this smell."

THERE'S DIRT IN YOUR EYE

After Nick and Judy caught the dingo who'd stolen the stinky cheese, Chief Bogo had put them right back on traffic duty. Today, they were watching for speeders on the almost-empty Meadowlands Highway, which was fine with Nick. He was still thinking about the cheese case. As a former criminal, he understood the criminal mind. But the dingo's mind was a mystery to him.

"So the dingo stole the cheese, drove out of town, and threw it over the prison wall because . . ." Nick pointed the radar gun out the window at the passing traffic.

"You need to attend our post-arrest interviews, Nick," Judy said. "He explained that he was trying to wow his lady friend with that fancy cheese. The price tag *is* pretty impressive. But she hated the smell, so he threw it out."

"Why at the prison, though?"

"He said the prisoners deserved the stink more than his neighbors. That's almost thoughtful, in a way."

Nick wrinkled his nose. "Seems like a lot of work just to get rid of cheese. But we solved the case. Too bad Chief Bogo put us back on traffic duty."

"If I find us a new case, will you stop whining?" Judy asked, partly because she was itching for another case herself. She radioed headquarters. "Clawhauser? Got any cases no one else wants that the chief wouldn't mind us investigating?"

"Let's see, Hopps. You know, one just came in. I'll ask the chief if he's okay with you taking it." There was a brief silence, and then the radio crackled. "You're good to go! Someone dumped dirt into the bay off the Old Outback Bridge."

"But that bridge is still being built," Judy said.

"No, I'm talking about the *old* bridge. Not that new Bridge to Everywhere that everyone's talking about—the crummy old bridge. The dirt landed—*kerplop!*—on a boatload of tourists taking a harbor cruise!"

"Thanks, Clawhauser," Judy said. It was her job to protect the citizens of Zootopia—even from dirt.

Just north of Savanna Central, there was a small beach. It was often full of animals sunning themselves. Boat tours around Zootopia launched from the nearby dock. A quarter mile north, a little street led to a decaying bridge. It crossed the water to Outback Island.

Judy parked beside the rickety staircase that led to a rickety dock under the rickety bridge. She understood now why they called it the *Old* Outback Bridge. It needed updating.

Judy and Nick approached a small tourist boat full of dusty sheep. They had been waiting to give their statements. "Baaaad way to start the day. Very baaaad." One of the sheep shook her woolly head, flinging dirt around. "One minute we were enjoying the sights, looking at the Zootopia skyline, and the next—" She twirled, showing off her dusty coat. "Need I say more?"

"Any idea who did this?" Nick asked. The sheep all shrugged.

"We were looking at the city, not the bridge," one said.

"By the time the dust cleared, the bridge was empty," said another.

"Does that bridge even go anywhere?" asked a third.

The guide cleared his throat and motioned for everyone to look east.

"The Old Outback Bridge leads to Outback Island, which is a quaint community of kangaroos, wallabies, wombats, dingoes . . ."

As the guide finished his talk about the island, Judy and Nick found the dumpsite. They walked up to the two-lane bridge to see if there were any clues. Sure enough, a small pile of dirt sat on the railing. Nick picked up a handful and let it sift through his fingers. Then he sniffed the rail.

"What is it?" Judy asked.

"I thought my sniffer was permanently disabled after all that stinky cheese, but I think I smell something. Perfume? Cologne?" He bent closer and spied a sparkling stone. "And there's this." He held it up, along with a few strands of fur.

"A common rhinestone and some fur." Judy squinted. She'd compare it to the fur sample kit she kept in her trunk. She held open an evidence bag. Nick put the fur and the rhinestone inside.

Nick jutted his thumb toward the shore of Outback Island, where a café overlooked the bridge. "Want to go see if someone in the restaurant saw the crime?"

Judy nodded. "If not, they might have a security camera that did."

Back at the car, she checked the fur against the samples in her kit. It matched kangaroo fur. Judy made a note of it, and then they crossed the bridge to Outback Island.

The restaurant was called Sheila's Café, and everyone who worked there was a marsupial. The koala and kangaroo waitresses carried straws and extra napkins in their pouches, which seemed very handy. Right now, those waitresses were sitting around since the café was nearly empty.

"Two for lunch?" the koala waitress greeted them. Her name tag read SHEILA: OWNER.

"We're just here for information," Judy said, flashing her badge.

"Lunch couldn't hurt," Nick said,

rubbing his belly. Maybe they'd get more information that way.

"Well, okay," Judy said. They followed the koala to a table.

She handed them menus. "I'm so glad you've decided to stay. Business has been slow since that new bridge was started. People forget about this island sometimes." She pasted a smile on her face. "Don't listen to me, though—take a look at the menu! I'll be back with some water and to answer your questions in a moment."

After Nick picked out his entrée, he turned to Judy. "Is this even a crime? Folks throw dirt into water all the time."

"It's not littering," Judy said, "but dumping anything off a bridge is unsafe. It could've blinded those sheep."

Sheila returned just then. "Someone

was dumping things off the bridge?"

"We were wondering if you saw anything. It happened a little while ago," Judy said.

Sheila shook her head. "Sorry, mate. What can I get you two?"

After they'd ordered and their meals had been served, Nick kept sniffing the air. Finally, he said, "Judy, can you please close the evidence bag? That smell is distracting me from my sandwich."

"I left it in the car," she said.

Nick sniffed again. He followed a scent across the café to where a kangaroo waitress was playing with her phone. He paused, leaned casually against the booth, and twitched his nose toward her.

Finally, the waitress looked up. "Can I help you?" she asked.

"Excuse me," he said, "can you tell me where you got your perfume?"

The waitress smiled. "Do you like it? It's called Eau de Outback. I picked it up today at the Marsupial Marketplace."

"Eau de Outback," Nick said. "Smells nice." He returned to the booth. "Hurry up, Carrots, we've got a lead!"

Judy continued to cut her lunch into small pieces. "You have the name of a perfume. For all you know, every female marsupial on Outback Island wears it. It's a great lead, but it will still be there in five minutes."

Finally, Judy finished her food, paid, and got directions to the Marsupial Marketplace along with the change. Soon they were at the market. Judy felt a little out of place among kangaroos, wallabies, koalas, and wombats. She envied Nick's ability to blend in with the Outbackers.

"Free perfume sample?" A salesperson at the counter of a kiosk held up a bottle. "It just came out today!" Before Nick could say no, the wallaby sprayed the bottle, and Nick walked right into the mist.

"So sorry," the wallaby said.

Nick was about to give her a piece of his mind. But then he stopped and sniffed. Then he sniffed again. "Just came out today?" he asked.

"Yes," the wallaby said. "And we're the only place in town that carries it. It's called Eau de Outback."

Nick turned to Judy. "Just came out today, Hopps. This scent is brand-new. And it's only sold here."

Judy spotted an overhead camera. "Can you please point us to security?" she asked the wallaby, who frowned, knowing she was not going to make a sale. Still, she pointed toward a corner office.

Officer Charles, a wombat, cooperated when Judy and Nick flashed their badges, pulling up security footage from that morning. They watched the wallaby making sales to all sorts of Outback animals. But they focused on finding the kangaroo in rhinestones. Finally, they spotted her.

Nick pointed triumphantly at the screen. "There she is," Nick told the security guard as they watched the kangaroo pay for the bottle of Eau de Outback and put it in her pouch. "Do you have outdoor cameras?"

"Absolutely." Charles punched some keys, and there was the kangaroo, moving toward her car. Officer

Charles zoomed in on the license plate.

Judy wrote it down. "Let's go pay a visit to Ms. Eau de Outback."

According to the police license plate database, the kangaroo's real name was Dorothy. She lived on Didgeridoo Avenue, a large neighborhood on the north side of the island.

Judy pulled out her badge and knocked on Dorothy's door. "Open up. Police." Dorothy came to the door. She smelled like Eau de Outback and was wearing a rhinestone jacket.

Nick pulled the rhinestone out of the evidence bag. "Does this belong to you?" he asked.

"No," the kangaroo said quickly. But

her hand crept up to cover an empty spot on the pocket of her jacket.

"Lower your hand, please," said Nick. Once she did, they could see the space where a rhinestone had been. She was clearly trying to hide something.

Judy cleared her throat. "Ma'am, have you been dumping dirt off the Old Outback Bridge?"

"Uh . . . um . . ." Dorothy stalled. "I mean, yes, I spilled some dirt by accident." She pointed toward her backyard. "Starting a garden. The bag of dirt was a little heavy. I bought it in the Rainforest District. They have great mulch. I was carrying it across the bridge, and I lost my balance and dropped it."

Judy pulled Nick aside. "We can't arrest her for that. Let's give her a warning," Judy whispered.

Nick agreed and returned to Dorothy. "Next time, you might want to take your car." He nodded at her. "Have a good day."

As they drove away, Judy frowned. "After all our hard work . . . it was just a clumsy gardener?"

Nick agreed that it wasn't much of a case. "Between this and the stinky cheese, it seems like detective work isn't very glamorous."

"I suppose you're right," Judy said. She radioed Clawhauser to tell him the case was solved, and that they were on their way back to headquarters to fill out their report.

Nick and Judy shared a fist bump. After all, this was the second day in a row they'd solved a case!

NO NOISE IS
GOOD NOISE

On her day off, Judy heated up a carrot casserole and thought about how she would explore Zootopia that afternoon. The TV played a clip from a reporter standing on Outback Island with a crowd of angry Outbackers behind her. Judy recognized the beach in front of Sheila's Café.

"The residents of Outback Island are upset about the Bridge to Everywhere. It's supposed to be completed next month and bypass Outback Island." Behind the reporter was a sign reading THE BRIDGE TO EVERYWHERE EXCEPT

OUTBACK ISLAND! The plans for the bridge flashed on the screen: a long stretch of road about fifty feet to the west of the island and fifty feet in the air. It had no on- or off-ramps.

"The residents of Outback Island have always felt isolated, but being excluded from 'everywhere,' as the name indicates, is the last straw. The protests, begun last summer by the infamous platypus—"

Judy turned off the TV. She bit into her food and wondered what Nick was doing.

Like Judy, Nick kept thinking of the cases. He had stopped by the prison, now mostly odor free, to see an old friend.

As he strolled away from the prison, he came to a strip mall in the nearby town. It had a drug store, a hoof-and-claw salon, a dry cleaner's, and a café on the edge of an alley. He paused to read the sign outside the café: PRIVATE PARTY EVERY DAY FROM NOON TO TWO. BACK TO REGULAR HOURS NEXT WEEK! Nick glanced at his watch. It was 11:59 on the dot.

A few bandicoots slunk into the café.
As the door opened, music exploded
onto the street, so loud it made Nick
jump. He couldn't help but stare. The
wolf who owned the dry cleaner's stuck
his long nose out the door.

"Keep it down!" he yelled, but he

seemed to know no one could hear him. He glanced at Nick and rolled his eyes. "At least this is the last day that horrible band will be performing. Good riddance!"

It was a horrible band; Nick had to agree. More of the strip mall's store owners had gathered to shake their fists at the café's dusty windows.

Even with the cafe doors closed, the music blared. "Bad for business," one store owner muttered.

"I wish the police would send an officer," said another. "They've been saying they're too busy for days!"

Police? Nick's ears pricked up. He didn't know if loud music was a crime, but he knew someone who would. And if it was . . . well, he was a crime fighter.

Nick pulled out his cell phone and

jogged a few blocks away so he could hear. He dialed Judy. "Carrots, it's Nick. I've got some questions about the law." He knew she'd never miss a chance to teach him. He told her where to meet him, then sat down on the curb to wait.

"What's that sound?" Judy asked when she got there.

"That's why I asked you to come," Nick said. He explained the music and the store owners' problem. "So . . . is loud music a crime?"

"It's called disturbing the peace," Judy said, "and we can definitely issue a warning."

"Better than nothing," Nick said.

The pair walked back to the strip

mall. Judy winced as her sensitive ears took in the sound. They peered in the café's window together. In the dim light, they saw animals gathered around tables and a crowd dancing in front of a stage. "You go tell the store owners we're on it," Judy said, "and I'll see if I can get them to turn down the music."

Judy stuck two cotton balls in her ears. She liked music, but it had to be good music. She pushed open the door . . . and immediately knew something wasn't right. The café was cheerful, with bright flowers and vintage décor. But there were trails of dirt all over the room. The band was even stranger. A group stood on the stage, pounding away on instruments. But the guitar was being held backward, and the keyboardist was playing upside down. The drummer was tapping his claws on a hideous yellow-green set of drums. None of the musicians seemed to care what the others were doing.

Yet in front of the stage, dozens of animals danced to a beat that didn't exist. Some even wore head lamps set on strobe. Weirder still, the two giant speakers had fallen over and were pointed down into the floor. That had caused a scratchy sort of tone to the noise, almost like paws scraping in the dirt.

The animals who weren't dancing had turned to frown at Judy. She walked over to a table of wombats playing cards. "Cool party," she said. "But don't you think the music is a little loud?"

One of the wombats frowned at her. "This isn't your kind of place," he said.

"This is Zootopia, a place where anyone can fit in anywhere," she said.

Another wombat snorted. "Tell that to the bridge builders."

The bridge? Judy frowned and looked around the café again. This time, she realized the guests were all Outbackers, clear across Zootopia from Outback Island. "The Old Outback Bridge is

perfectly lovely," Judy said. "Why, I was just on it yesterday."

"Lovely and falling apart," a wombat said grumpily. "Don't pretend you understand, bunny."

Judy tried to think of something optimistic to say, but feeling the tension, she just waved goodbye. She didn't like it when Zootopia was split between animal groups.

"They're not listening to me," she said to Nick when they met up on the sidewalk in front of the dry cleaner's. "That café is an Outbacker hangout. With the bridge drama, they're feeling passed over, ignored. I'm not an Outbacker, so they won't talk to me."

A dingo entered the café as if to prove her point. Then Nick's eyes lit up. "You're not an Outbacker," he said, "but I could pass for a dingo." He jammed sunglasses on his face.

Judy eyed him. "That almost works. You'll have to hide your tail, though—it's kind of too fluffy for a dingo." She peered through a window. "I'll watch from here."

Seconds later, Nick plopped down at the counter. He also took in the strange trails of dirt, the weird band, and the collapsed speakers.

"Root beer, please," Nick ordered. He brushed some dirt off the counter.

"What kind of dingo are you, mate?" a dingo to Nick's left asked.

"Yeah," said the bartender, "did you shrink in the dryer?"

Nick laughed. "Shrunk in the dryer, that's a good one, mate. I just washed my fur, and I can't do a thing with it." But the dingo didn't laugh. Nick hurried on. "I heard about this place from my pal Charles. Great guy . . . wombat. We've worked in security for a while now. The guy's always up for a party. But the middle of the day is a strange time for a party."

Nick's tail twitched, and the dingo saw it. "That isn't a dingo tail," he said. "Looks more like something you'd see . . . on a fox. Hey, you're not an Outbacker. Why are you here?"

A couple more dingoes came up behind Nick and loomed over him. He put his paws up. The band kept playing, but no one was dancing anymore.

"Why are you here?" the dingo asked again.

"Uh . . . I—I've always wished I were a dingo," Nick stammered knowing he

was surrounded and not wanting to cause any trouble. He hoped Judy was watching from outside.

"Zootopia police! Step away from him!" Judy burst into the room, holding her badge in one hand and stun gun in the other.

The dingoes backed away with their hands up. "Easy with that," one of them said, nervously eyeing the stun gun.

"Just in the nick of time," Nick muttered.

Judy called for the owner of the café. A Tasmanian devil came out from the back, looking nervous. "What can I do for you, Officer?"

Nick explained that the other store owners in the strip mall were losing business over the loud music. "You're disturbing the peace," he said.

Strangely, the Tasmanian devil looked relieved. "It's my nephew's band," he explained. "They're awful, but I promised him they could play here for one week. It's good for my business. He brought all his friends, and he's got a lot of friends. Tell you what. I'll have all these patrons go visit the other stores, too. Make some purchases, make up for driving away business. And after today, the band will stop. Sound good?"

Nick took a step and tripped on a pile of dirt. Judy frowned. "That sounds good," she said, "but we'll be sending a health inspector tomorrow about all this dirt. You can't run a restaurant like this." They nodded to the owner, and looked at the Outbackers who'd already returned to the band and were shaking their fur on the dirty dance floor.

"Not my kind of place," Judy said as they walked back to her car.

Nick brushed some dirt off his arm. "Mine either."

"Outbackers are awfully upset about that bridge," Judy said. "I hate seeing Zootopia divided like this."

"Me too," said Nick.

THE DIG'S UP

On a sunny day in Zootopia, Judy and Nick were back on traffic duty on the Meadowlands Highway. Because it was such a flat, open stretch of road, animals usually drove pretty fast.

"Outback Island has been keeping us busy lately," Nick said. "The dingo with the cheese, the kangaroo gardener, and now the party animals. What do you think is going on?"

"They're probably acting up because of the bridge," Judy said. "But the cases don't seem to be connected."

"True," Nick said. "But back when I

was 'legally adjacent,' nothing was ever a coincidence. And there are too many coincidences between these cases."

The police radio crackled to life. "Hopps, Wilde," came Clawhauser's voice. "There's been a prison break. You're the closest officers, and the chief wants ZPD on the scene as soon as possible."

Judy snatched her radio gleefully, happy for once to be on traffic duty in the middle of nowhere. "Hopps and Wilde, on the case!"

Nick flipped on the siren and floored the gas pedal, shooting down the highway. They passed the strip mall, now calm and quiet. Seconds later, they arrived at the prison.

They hurried in and met the warden in a cell on the west side. He was stringing police tape around a hole in the floor.

Judy pulled out her carrot pen and a pad of paper while Nick examined the hole.

"Glad you could make it," said the warden. "Right now we're trying to contain things and keep the other prisoners from finding out about this. If they know escape's possible, they might try it themselves."

"Who's the escapee?" asked Judy.

"A pesky platypus."

"The same one who had to be relocated because of the cheese?" Judy asked.

The warden nodded. "Name of Singcor Swim. His accomplices wouldn't have been able to tunnel into solitary, but when he was moved because of the cheese, they were able to tunnel up into the cells here on the west side. This side of the prison is older. No reinforced cement in the ground."

Nick held up a few strands of fur and gave them a sniff. "Can't tell the animal," he said.

"Let's check the kit," said Judy. In the trunk of the police car, they found a match quickly: wombat. Judy fetched two head lamps and they went back inside the prison. "Let's see where this trail goes!"

Nick waved away the lamp and jumped

inside. Judy had forgotten he could see in the dark. She put on her head lamp and followed him.

The tunnel went on and on. It was barely big enough for Nick. Dirt was falling on them from the sides. Finally, it ended in a sewer. "All this digging," Nick said, "and nobody heard it?"

Judy scampered ahead. She looked around. "Well, if they did their digging between noon and two, nobody would hear much of anything."

"You mean . . ." Nick hurried to join her. The tunnel ended in an alley behind the strip mall—right behind the café they had investigated the day before. Judy and Nick had sent a health inspector to shut it down for being full of dirt.

"Nobody heard digging," said Nick, "because they heard loud, terrible music."

"That explains the dirt," Judy said, remembering the dirty floors and tables. "They had to take it out through the restaurant. It also explains why the partiers were wearing head lamps, and why I thought I heard scratching. But

where did they dump all of the dirt?"

Nick climbed out of the hole, sniffed, and peered into a nearby Dumpster. "No dirt in here," he said, frowning. Then he spied something in the corner and reached in.

"But if you dig a tunnel that long, the dirt has got to go somewhere," Judy said.

Nick held up a perfume bottle triumphantly. "I've smelled this perfume before! This was the same scent that kangaroo was wearing when she threw the dirt off the bridge! Hey! Do you think—"

Judy jumped in. "Kangaroos have pouches. They could've carried the dirt away without anyone seeing anything!"

Nick leapt out of the Dumpster. "I think we need to pay our friend Dorothy a visit again. She's probably been working with friends."

Judy pointed to tire tracks in the dirt. "They had a vehicle waiting. Maybe someone saw something."

They headed to the dry cleaner's and asked the wolf owner if he had seen anything. "Just a bunch of Outbackers driving off. Even a platypus! You don't see his type around here often," he said. "They went down the Meadowlands Highway, toward Zootopia."

Judy and Nick thanked the wolf, then hurried to the prison to fetch their car. They needed to question Dorothy the kangaroo.

"Hopps," said Nick, "remember when I said that nothing was ever a coincidence?"

"Yes, I do." She was tapping away on her laptop. "You were right. Everything is coming together. Hey, look at this."

"I'm driving."

"Oh, right. I've got Singcor Swim's rap sheet here onscreen. It says he's the founder of O.F.E."

"Oaf?" asked Nick.

"Outbackers for Equality. That sounds like a good cause," said Judy. "I believe in equality."

Nick shook his head. "Singcor Swim uses the group to organize some not-so-peaceful protests. He once drove a truck into a wall at city hall after a newspaper misprint; the writer mistook a wallaby for a small kangaroo. And that's just one of his protests in the name of equality."

"No wonder they locked him away," Judy said.

Judy and Nick drove up the bay and crossed the Old Outback Bridge. They parked in front of Dorothy's house and went to the door. Judy knocked loudly. "Police. We have a few questions."

But there was no answer.

She knocked again. Then again.

"Let's look around back," Nick said, already halfway around the house.

Judy followed Nick. The place was deserted.

A detached garage stood in the backyard with its door wide open.

"Let's take a peek," Nick said.

"Without a search warrant?"

"The door is open," Nick pointed out.

Inside the garage, there was a large table with a dozen chairs around it. But no sign of Dorothy the kangaroo . . . or anyone else. Nick sniffed. "Eau de Outback, for sure. But we already knew she lived here."

Wind blew through the garage, and Judy's ears twitched. She heard a few musical notes. She followed the sound to a corner of the garage and pulled back a tarp. "The instruments from the café!" she exclaimed. The breeze had ruffled the guitar's strings. She would recognize the hideous yellow-green drum set anywhere.

"Good work," said Nick. "This must be their headquarters."

"Then why leave? If you break out of prison, you stay hidden." Judy sat in one of the chairs and looked over at Nick.

"You stay put until the heat's off. Unless . . ." Nick picked up a square of wood with words painted on it. "Unless you're on a mission."

He held up the sign for Judy to see: THE BRIDGE TO EVERYWHERE EXCEPT OUTBACK ISLAND!

They found a stack of signs on the floor. Judy remembered seeing the newscast on television about Outbackers protesting the bridge—and these looked like the same signs!

"Bridge protestors," Judy said. "They must have broken Singcor Swim out of prison. But why?"

"We need to get to the bridge," Nick said, running to their car. He hopped in the driver's seat and turned on the siren and the flashing lights. "I love this part of the job."

"Chasing the bad guys?" Judy asked.

"No, turning on the siren."

Soon they had crossed the Old Outback Bridge and were on the mainland. Right now, the bridge was about three-quarters finished. It looked spooky in the dusky light.

Construction was done for the day. But as they drove closer, they could see a few cement trucks parked by the water's edge as well as one truck parked halfway down the incomplete bridge. Nick screeched to a stop outside the construction zone, and he and Judy jumped the fence.

Inside, by the entrance to the bridge,

a group of Outbackers were gathering a stack of signs. Judy recognized Dorothy and a couple of dingoes who'd been in the café. There was no sign of Singcor Swim.

"What's going on here?" Judy asked. The dingoes tensed. "This is a restricted area."

Behind her, Nick quietly radioed for reinforcements.

"Why?" challenged Dorothy. "Because we're Outbackers who dare to be on the mainland? We belong here as much as you do!"

"Yeah!" chorused the others.

"No," Judy said, "because it's a dangerous construction site that isn't safe to be standing on."

"This bridge should include us!" Dorothy said. "The Old Outback

Bridge is falling apart, and what do the politicians do?"

"They build a new bridge that goes somewhere *else*!" yelled a dingo.

"That's right! It's the Bridge to Everywhere—except where?" Dorothy riled up the crowd.

"Except Outback Island!" they replied.

Dorothy turned back to Nick and Judy. "I could hop to the new bridge from the island, but I shouldn't have to. They should have built on- and off-ramps for us."

Judy stepped forward to address the Outbackers who stood to the side of the road. She wasn't sure what she was going to say yet, but she had to calm them down. But then, the ground began to shake. Something deep and rumbly, like a—

"Look out!" Nick yelled. He threw himself at Judy, knocking her out of the way just as a huge cement truck rumbled past. Singcor Swim was behind the wheel, eyes narrowed in concentration. He turned around for another pass, one that would take him up and across the new bridge.

This time Judy saw it coming and leapt onto the truck's hood. She climbed to the open window and drew her stun gun from its holster. She pointed it at Singcor Swim.

"Stop this truck!" she yelled.

Singcor Swim reached for something beside him on the seat. But before he got to it, Judy pulled the trigger.

Zap!

The charge missed the platypus, but Singcor Swim was so surprised that he yanked the steering wheel. The huge cement truck, along with Judy, careened through the guardrails and plunged into the bay.

"Carrots!" Nick ran toward the water, searching frantically for his partner.

There was no sign of the truck. Suddenly Singcor Swim popped to the surface, pulling Judy next to him. With his flat, beaver-like tail, he brought her to the shallows. Nick splashed into the water and helped the platypus bring his partner to shore.

Lying on the sand, Judy coughed and shook water out of her ears. Then she jumped to her feet. "You're under arrest!" she exclaimed, pointing at the platypus. Nick snapped cuffs on his wet wrists.

"Under arrest is better than under the Bridge to Everywhere," the platypus said.

"That bridge crosses right next to and above Outback Island. I thought Zootopia was supposed to be for all animals. So why did they forget Outback Island?"

"I see your point," Judy said, wringing her still-soggy ears. "But breaking out of prison? Stealing a cement truck? Trying to run over cops? There are other ways to go about this."

"What were you going to do with the cement truck?" Nick asked.

"I was going to drive it into the bay, along with the rest of the materials, so they couldn't finish the bridge. That way they couldn't bypass us. That way they would have to remember we exist."

Sirens blared and a helicopter whirled overhead as the news reporters and police backup arrived. "Now they won't forget you any time soon," said Judy.

While Judy leaned against the squad car with a blanket over her shoulders, other officers rounded up the rest of the bridge protestors. "So you were right. The cases were related, after all," she said to Nick.

Nick nodded. "The dingo stole the stinky cheese and threw it over the prison wall on purpose, so Singcor Swim would get moved to a part of the prison that was easier to dig into. The café was a cover for the tunnel into the prison . . . and Dorothy was getting rid of the dirt by hiding it in her pouch and dumping it in the bay." Nick shook his head. "I almost admire that platypus—it was a good hustle."

"Imagine if Singcor Swim went about

this legally," Judy said. "He's smart enough to accomplish anything he wants."

As they discussed the case over the next few days, Nick and Judy decided to make sure the island's residents weren't ignored. But they needed help, so they jumped into the car for a quick visit to Sheila.

"After all that hullabaloo, I'm surprised to see you two," she said.

Nick gave her a piece of paper. "We want to help," he said.

She looked down at the paper and saw a name and a phone number. "Vince Mousawitz?" she asked.

"He wants to run for mayor. And we helped him get his stinky cheese back. If he assists the Outbackers, he figures he would have all of your votes."

Sheila smiled. "Yes, yes, he would."

Vince did help the Outbackers, and at last count, was leading in the polls. Because that's the way it should be in Zootopia, where everyone belonged and everyone got along . . .

Most of the time.